LITTLE LIBRARY · NUMBER THREE

CONSTANCE MARKIEVICZ

JOHN & FATTI BURKE

GILL BOOKS

onstance Gore-Booth was born in 1868. She grew up with her brothers and sisters in Lissadell House in Sligo. Her father was a wealthy landlord who was good to his tenants.

Constance had a dream. She wanted Ireland to be free and its people to be treated fairly.

Connie, as she was known by her friends and family, was brave and adventurous. She loved horse riding and hunting and painting. Her best friend was her sister Eva, who wrote poetry and plays.

When she was 19, Connie went to Paris to study art. There she met a Polish Count called Casimir Markievicz. They got married and settled in Dublin where they worked in theatre. Their daughter, Maeve, was raised in Lissadell.

Constance joined Cumann na mBan, a women's group that wanted freedom for Ireland. She also co-founded a boy-scout brigade called Na Fianna Éireann, where boys were trained to fight for Ireland.

In her old motor car, she would bring the boys camping in the Wicklow hills. Though she was often seen underneath her car doing repairs!

Constance also joined the
Suffragettes, who wanted women
to have the right to vote. They
protested King George V's visit
to Ireland, where Constance
was arrested and sent to prison.
But when she was released, she
continued her work!

In 1913 there was a big strike in Dublin known as the Dublin Lock-out. It lasted a really long time because the bosses wouldn't give in, so the poorest families went hungry.

James Connolly organised the Irish Citizen Army to protect the workers, and Constance joined them. She even designed their uniforms.

Constance set up a soup
kitchen using her own money.
She brought food and supplies
to the tenements, and often
dragged bags of fuel up the
stairs. The people loved her
and called her 'Madam'.

Rebellion was in the air. In 1914 guns were smuggled into Howth Harbour on board a ship called the *Asgard*, and Constance and her boys helped to unload the weapons.

The Rising began on Easter Monday 1916. Constance made the green flag that flew over the GPO.

She fought with the Irish Citizen Army in St Stephen's Green where snipers shot at them. But Constance returned fire.

They moved to the College of Surgeons where they fought for six days until they had to surrender. The leaders were brought to Kilmainham Gaol and were sentenced to death.

Most of the leaders were executed, including
Pádraig Pearse, Tom Clarke, Joseph Plunkett,
Thomas MacDonagh and Constance's good friend
James Connolly. Because she was a woman,
Constance was not executed, but she was sent to
prison in Britain with hundreds of other fighters.

In 1917 all the remaining prisoners were released, including Constance.

They came back to Ireland as heroes and got a huge welcome. There was lots of celebration and a big parade!

The following year, women won the right to vote.
At the next election, 73 Sinn Féin members were
successfully elected, including Constance.

She was the first
woman to be elected to
the British parliament
but she would not take
her seat. Instead, Sinn
Féin set up their own
parliament in Dublin
called the Dáil, with
Constance as Minister
for Labour.

The Dáil was illegal and meetings were held in secret. Constance had no home now so she moved from place to place, staying with friends.

One evening she heard that the police were coming, so she put all her documents into a trunk and hid it in the window of a furniture shop. Luckily the police didn't spot it!

Peace finally came in 1921. A treaty was signed and Ireland became a Free State, but not a Republic. Many people were not happy about this and a civil war started.

1921
ANGLO-IRISH
TREATY

Constance travelled around the country speaking out against the treaty. One day, while starting her car, she broke her arm. But that didn't stop her.

'I'm glad it wasn't my jaw I broke,' she said.
'I can still talk!'

The civil war ended and the Free State won. Constance joined Éamon de Valera's new Fianna Fáil party and she was elected again. But Constance never got a chance to take her seat in the Dáil.

She became very ill and was rushed to hospital. This brave and generous lady died poor but happy, surrounded by the people she loved.

She lived to see the beginning of her dream of a free and fair Ireland.

Timeline

1868
Constance is born
on 4 February

1898
She goes to Paris
to study art

1900
Constance marries Count
Casimir Markievicz

1901
Her daughter
Maeve is born

1909
Constance co-founds
Na Fianna Éireann with
Bulmer Hobson

1911
She is arrested
while protesting against
the visit of King George V

1913
Constance organises soup
kitchens in the Dublin
slums and at Liberty Hall
during the lock-out

1916
She is arrested after
the Easter Rising and
sent to Aylesbury
Prison in England

1921
Ceasefire and the Anglo-Irish Treaty

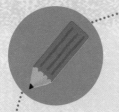

1922
Civil War begins and Constance sides with the Republicans

1923
End of the Civil War – Republicans lose

1919
Constance is elected to Westminster Parliament and the War of Independence starts

VOTE
14 DECEMBER 1918
MARKIEVICZ

1926
Constance joins a new political party called Fianna Fáil

1918
She is accused of plotting against the British during World War I and sent to prison

VÓTÁIL

1927
She is elected again to the Dáil in June

1917
Constance is released and comes home to a great welcome in Ireland

1927
Constance becomes ill and dies on 15 July. She is buried at Glasnevin Cemetery after a massive funeral

Did You Know?

A number of PLACES are named after Constance Markievicz. These include government office blocks, housing estates, a sports centre and MARKIEVICZ PARK, the headquarters of Sligo GAA.

There is a FINE STATUE of Constance Markievicz by John Coll in RATHCORMACK, Co. Sligo. There is a bust of her in ST STEPHEN'S GREEN and a lovely statue of Constance and her dog Poppet in TARA STREET in Dublin.

When her death sentence was changed to LIFE IMPRISONMENT, she is reported to have said, 'I do wish your lot had the decency to shoot me.'

During the WORKER'S STRIKE, Constance took out many loans to HELP THE CAUSE. She also sold all her jewellery.

In May 1926 the FIRST MEETING OF FIANNA FÁIL at the La Scala Theatre in Dublin was chaired by Constance, with Éamon de Valera as party leader.

Na Fianna Éireann was mostly for boys but there was also a GIRL'S BRIGADE in Belfast. They came down to the south in the summer for training. Many of these girls were later active in CUMANN NA MBAN.

Constance's HUSBAND Casimir Markievicz was a Polish playwright, theatre director and painter. He founded the Independent Dramatic Company in Dublin where he wrote plays in which Constance starred.

Beautiful LISSADELL HOUSE, now owned by the Cassidy-Walsh family, is open to the public and provides guided tours of the house as well as visits to its wonderful gardens and exhibitions.

When asked for advice on how a lady should dress in those days, Constance said, 'Dress suitably in SHORT SKIRTS and STRONG BOOTS, leave your JEWELS in the bank and buy a REVOLVER.'

When Constance died, the Free State Government refused to give her a STATE FUNERAL. Her body was laid in a cinema (the Rotunda) where 100,000 people filed past. An estimated 300,000 people lined the streets as her body was taken to GLASNEVIN CEMETERY.

Her PRISON TERMS included periods in Aylesbury Prison (August 1916–June 1917), Holloway Prison (1918–1919), Cork City Gaol (June 1919–October 1919), Mountjoy Prison (October 1920–June 1921) and North Dublin Union Internment Camp (1923).

Constance's father Henry was an ARCTIC EXPLORER. He also wrote books about Arctic exploration, yachting and whaling.

ABOUT the AUTHORS

KATHI 'FATTI' BURKE is an Irish illustrator. She lives in Amsterdam.

JOHN BURKE is Fatti's dad. He is a retired primary school teacher and principal. He lives in Waterford.

Their first book, *Irelandopedia*, won *The Ryan Tubridy Show* Listeners' Choice Award at the Irish Book Awards 2015, and the Eilís Dillon Award for first children's book and the Judges' Special Award at the CBI Book of the Year Awards 2016. Their next books, *Historopedia* and *Foclóiropedia,* were nominated for the Specsavers Children's Book of the Year (Junior) Award at the Irish Book Awards 2016 and 2017. Their books have sold over 100,000 copies in Ireland.

ALSO in the LITTLE LIBRARY SERIES

BOOK ONE

BOOK TWO

ALSO by the AUTHORS

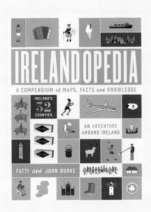

Gill Books

Hume Avenue

Park West

Dublin 12

www.gillbooks.ie

Gill Books is an imprint of M.H. Gill and Co.

Text © John Burke 2019

Illustrations © Kathi Burke 2019

978 07171 8455 2

Designed by www.grahamthew.com

Printed by L&C Group, Poland

This book is typeset in 13pt on 25pt Sofia Pro.

The paper used in this book comes from the wood pulp of managed forests. For every tree felled, at least one tree is planted, thereby renewing natural resources.

A CIP catalogue record for this book is available from the British Library.

5 4 3 2 1